IN THE NIGHT KITCHEN

MAURICE SENDAK

HARPER & ROW, PUBLISHERS

FOR SADIE AND PHILIP

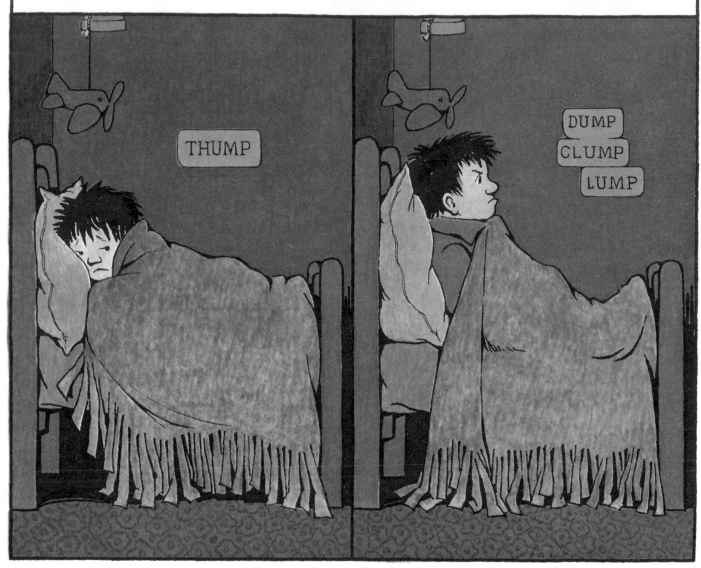

AND SHOUTED

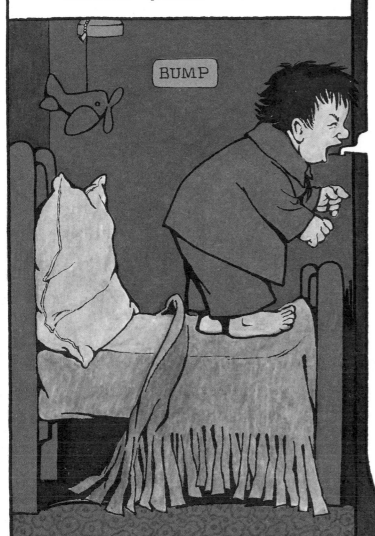

QUIET DOWN THERE!

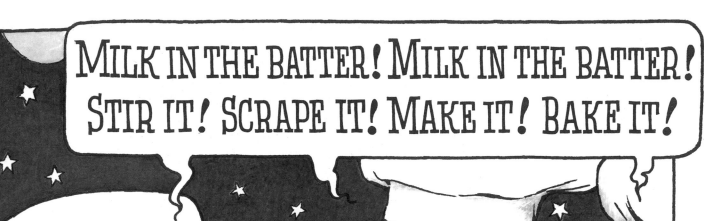

AND THEY PUT THAT BATTER UP TO BAKE

A DELICIOUS MICKEY-CAKE.

SO HE SKIPPED FROM THE OVEN & INTO BREAD DOUGH
ALL READY TO RISE IN THE NIGHT KITCHEN.

HE KNEADED AND PUNCHED IT
AND POUNDED AND PULLED

WHEN THE BAKERS RAN UP
WITH A MEASURING CUP, HOWLING:

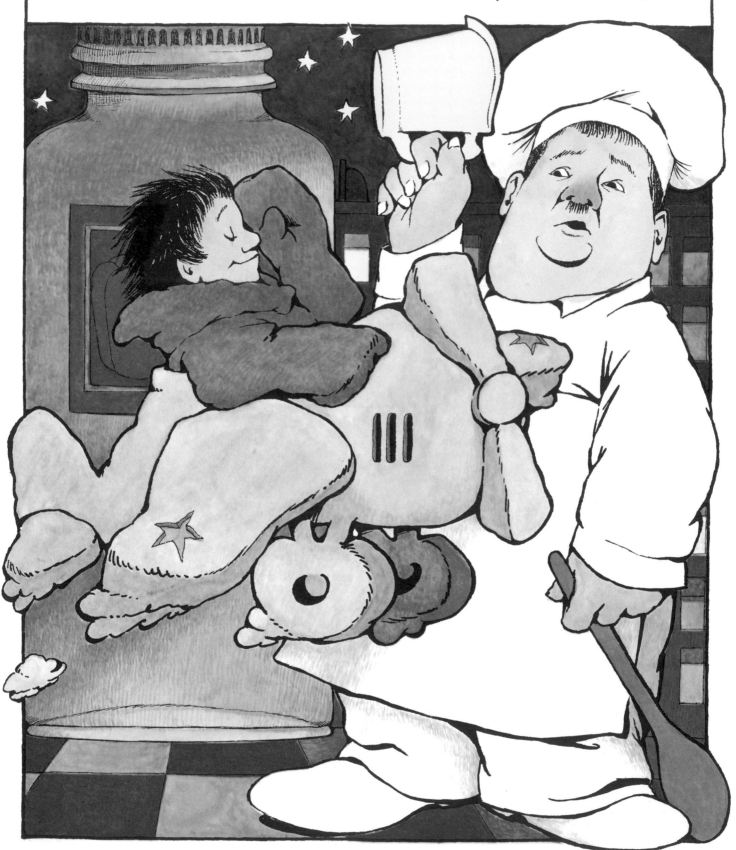

AND OVER THE TOP
OF THE MILKY WAY
IN THE NIGHT KITCHEN.

SO THE BAKERS THEY MIXED IT AND BEAT IT AND BAKED IT.

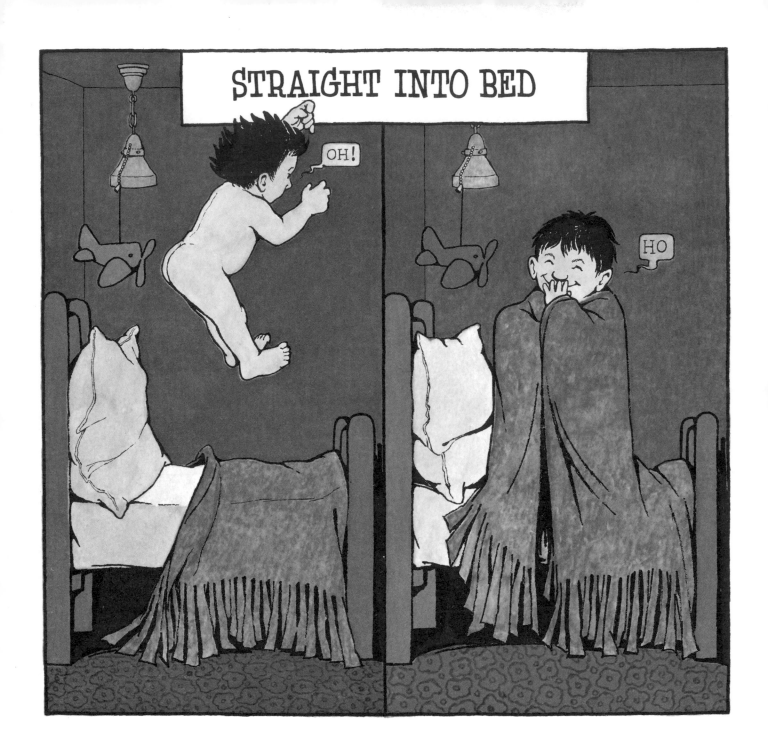